NIMI

THE WARRIOR

GIRL

ABIOSE FALADE AND **DAMILOLA OTUN**

NIMI: THE WARROR GIRL

WRITTEN BY
ABIOSE FALADE AND **DAMILOLA OTUN**
bfalade3@gmail.com   otundammy@gmail.com

ISBN: **978-978-991-858-4**

Published by:

COMMUNE WRITERS INT'L
www.communewriters.com
+234 8139 260 389
6, Amusa Street, Agodo-Egbe, Lagos

Published and Printed in the Federal Republic of Nigeria

DISCLAIMER

This novel is a work of fiction. Names, characters, places, and incidents are either the author's imagination or are used fictitiously. Any resemblance to actual events or locales or persons, living or dead, is entirely coincidental.

DEDICATION

I want to say a very big thank you to all the people who have stood by me all through my life. It has been really fun writing NIMI.

To God, the source of inspiration and the creator of all things, with breath and without.

Maami, thank you for always seeing the very best in me. For trying to understand me when sometimes I couldn't even understand myself.

Daddy, thank you for the strict upbringing, it made me stronger than anything else.

To my wonderful grandfather, I know you would be so proud of me in heaven. Pappy, thank you for teaching me to love God more than anything.

Professor Mike Adewunmi, thank you for giving me the idea that brought about Nimi: the warrior girl.

To my bestie, thank you for being my third biggest cheerleader, for being tough when needed. Thank you for reminding me that God is the best.

To Fola Asebiomo, thank you for helping me edit this project even when we all were sick.

To Damilola, thank you for being a wonderful
support.

PREFACE

I tell myself every day that I am not my disability. I speak words of affirmation to myself, build a world filled with my imaginations to get by the day. It was good, and I usually felt good after this routine. Later, it was not working anymore, and I consciously did many things to change my environment and blend in. My diet changed, my sleeping pattern. I thought I was a changed person and needed affirmations to get by. Affirmations are good and help ones self-esteem and confidence, but in my case, I was using the affirmations for a different thing I needed then; an environment change.

It took a long time before I learnt to deal with it better, and I discovered the problem was not particularly me; it was from my environment. I was accustomed to seeing disability as something bad. Movies, news, and culture depicted disability as a negative thing. I grew up among boys, and I watched Wrestlemania when others were watching Barbie. Marvel and DC movies were my own

Cinderella stories. I loved it. It was rare to see a superhero with a disability.

I was excited when Biose invited me to work on this project. There were stories we listened to as we grew up, Tales by moonlight. Africa has a lot of myths and folktales. I was excited to tell a story my children and grandchildren would love to hear, a story of an inclusive society. A society I hope we will be. I hope it warms your heart as it has mine, and I hope every child with or without disabilities finds the hero in them.

PROLOGUE

The priest visited the palace and asked that a village meeting be called. The King summoned an assembly of the village chiefs, elders, and citizens. The priest had received a series of prophecies from the gods and he needed to share them as soon as possible, for they weighed heavy on his heart.

As the people gathered, he stood tall, looked up to the heavens, and began to declare:

A time comes.

When people will be subjected to force and tyranny - they will be ruled by fear.

Women will be deprived of their children.

Babies abandoned by the river; left to die.

But they would be snatched from death's claws by an unknown spirit.

In a world filled with so much evil, he would train them to become a force of positive change.

Out of the undesirable, one will arise to change things around.

Another will rise to ease the pain.

A total of seven beings will rise.

They will transform the world and bring back its glory.

He paused and looked around. Eye to eye, he stared at each of the royals at the assembly. A number of them were seen squirming in discomfort. As though he was searching for answers, he looked to the East, then to the West, to the North, and the South. Then he drew a deep breath, and as he did previously, he gazed to the heavens and prophesied a second time. His voice was louder. The things he said were a little like the first:

In the time of tyranny, fear was enthroned.

There was gnashing of teeth and wailing under a cruel and oppressive government

Babies, still covered in blood, are torn from their mothers' arms.

The cries of babies make the river unapproachable.

No one knows what lies there.

No one is brave enough to find out.

Everyone is scared.

Who cares?!

Forever? No, this won't go on forever.

There will be a revolt, led by one of those who cry at the riverbank.

An army will rise, and all will follow their voice.

As soon as he stopped speaking, the clouds became dark. The heavens thundered. The people began to murmur among themselves. The elders chanted ancient panegyrics, imploring the gods to ward off disaster. Everyone was afraid to ask the priest what these things meant and when they would be. One after the other, talking in hushed tones, they walked away, back to their houses.

For months afterwards, people would congregate in clusters and talk about how strange the prophecy was.

1

THE SAVE

It was a quiet evening in the jungle; there was silence everywhere. No birds singing. All the animals were still. The only thing that could be heard was the shrill, piteous cry of a baby. "What could have made a mother drop her young child by the stream and walk away?" the animals wondered. As the animals wondered about this, the surface of the water stirred, ripples forming as a head broke the surface of the calm river. Out of the water came a young man with fluorescent skin, he had huge wings, dark as night, emerging from his shoulder blades. As he came out of the water, the animals got nervous and waited, peeping from hiding, wanting to see what was going to happen.

The man shook his head as he approached the wailing newborn.

"Again! When will these people learn? When will they stop sending gifts of salvation away from them? Thank Heaven that this one wasn't killed - that would have been a shame because... Oh well!. Where is that guardian I told to guard the river?"

Aja was the being who guarded both the river that the children with deformities were dropped at and the entire forest that surrounded it. Many times, mothers could not get themselves to reach the riverside before they had to separate themselves from their children - it broke their hearts. He often informed Malika about the developments at the riverside.

While he was yet speaking, there was a disturbance in the jungle, and out came *Aja*, the guardian of the forest. Aja was even bigger than Malika, the winged man standing by the riverside. With his large head, sharp teeth, and yellow eyes, Aja was truly terrifying to look at. Little wonder he was mandated to guard the forest to keep away those who often came to kill the babies.

"Ah! There you are, where were you? How did this happen?"

"Not again, another child has been dropped off by the riverbank", Aja mumbled.
"Let's be thankful that this one wasn't dropped on the pathway where a leopard or some other animal could eat it up immediately. Aseda, thank you o."

"Let's see what reasons they have this time", said the winged man. As he squatted near the child, his wings opened and cast a shadow on the baby. The baby, sensing people near, began to cry louder and they no longer had to guess why the newborn had been dropped - the child couldn't move both her legs; to make it worse, part of her upper body was twisted.

"*Aseda* o!" Aja screamed in shock.
Malika jumped. "What happened, why are you shouting?!"
Aja stuttered, "I was just… just shocked at the way she looks."
Malika looked up to the sky and wondered why Eledumare would choose such a guardian to help pick these children.

"So you needed to shout, because this was the first time you would see a deformed child?" Malika asked. "Is that what you're telling me?"
"Well, that's not what I'm saying. It's just that it's shocking sometimes when I see that they don't appreciate what they have due to fear," replied Aja.

The guardian turned to Malika, the fallen angel, and said: "Isn't this...? I am not sure. Let me check." *(The guardian and Malika remembered a prophecy that spoke of seven courageous undesirables that would change everything as they knew it.)*

Malika moved closer to the child and lifted the child's arm. That was when he saw the mark on the arm. The mark looked like a quarter moon, with bumps around it. Amazed, he turned around and murmured: "you are right, she is the child!" Shaking his head, he said: "When will they learn? When will they understand that their culture is there so that they can be saved from their hardship? Could it be that they don't know the prophecy? Or they don't believe that such is possible?"

With these questions lingering heavily on his mind, the fallen angel carried the child and turned around to go back to where he came from.

The guardian asked him, "Where are you going?" "Where else, but the Academy? Where again will I take the child, other than where she will be trained to fulfil her mission on earth?"

2

MANY YEARS BEFORE

[The Ancient Town of Ilaro]

The Baale of Ilaro was with his chiefs and the *Ifa* priest. The *Ifa* priest was seldom summoned to the palace, so everyone was concerned. Something had to be wrong for the Baale to summon the priest to the palace. People who were at the palace spoke in hushed tones and whispers. They wanted to know what was wrong. The Ifa priest listened as the Baale spoke.

"Wise one, I have been having dreams that are quite disturbing. In my dreams, I see a chair. This chair is golden, with precious stones surrounding it. Sitting on this chair is a young child, being carried around on this chair. This child always has a smile on her face, and the strangest thing about this dream is that I wasn't the Baale of this village! No, I wasn't! The child was the king and there was no Baale."

This dream shocked everyone in the courtyard of the palace because this kind of thing had never been known to happen. Could Ilaro finally have a Child-King, or was there a way that the current Baale could end up not being King? This worried the Baale so much that he asked the Ifa priest: "Wise one, what must I do to ensure that I become the king of this village?"

The *Ifa* priest replied: "you must ensure that you are always kind to everyone around you, and don't let anyone lack anything for as long as you are alive".

The Baale thanked the priest and gifted him some cowries.

After the *Ifa* priest left, the Baale began to pace up and down the throne room, talking to himself.

"This man must think that I am stupid; very stupid, if he thinks that he can tell me anything and I will believe, he is not serious. Baba Ifabiyi is the only person I trust to make sure I become king", he thought. "If this *Ifa* priest believes that I will do as he says, then he is mistaken, and seriously too."

The truth was that the Baale had not been meant to be the Baale. He had become the Baale by conniving and being devious. It had not been meant for him. Sadly, the man that was meant to be the Baale, Adewale, had been caught in a compromising position where he was found in bed with a three-year-old child who had blood on her. It happened that it was the new yam festival which meant there was a celebration in the land. Adewale had been in the company of his younger brother Adedeji celebrating the new yam festival.

"Happy festival, my elder brother", Shouted Adedeji with so much false joy in his voice

"Thank you my brother! May this new yam festival brings us good fortune."

"Ase!" shouted everyone who heard the prayer

" Come, let's celebrate!! Shouted Adewale with so much joy to be with his family and friends. If only he knew what was about to happen, he wouldn't have been so happy. As the day wore on, everyone was as intoxicated as was possible. Drinks were flowing freely, as everyone was in a joyful mood. As it got dark, Adedeji went into his brother's wife room and picked up their three-year-old daughter Adunni quietly and took her to her father's room, placing her in a way that would suggest rape with blood all over her.

This was considered an abomination of the highest order, and that was how the title passed over him.

As the Baale continued to pace the throne room, he thought of what he could do to hold on to the throne and not lose the kingship to another. That was when he got the idea that from then on, no child born deformed would be allowed to live. Because of the fear of his dream coming to pass and his quest for power, he rained terror on his people - he deprived mothers of their children.

One day, as the Baale was walking around his community, he came across an old man who walked past him without greeting him. The Baale was shocked beyond words. He shouted: "Old man! Why would you pass by me and not greet me? Am I so small or so insignificant?" The old man looked at him, from head to toe, and replied: "I am sorry, but I did not see anything special about you. All I saw was a dictator who feels overly important about himself."

The Baale opened his mouth in shock. When he finally recovered, he asked his guards to seize the old man and put him in prison, where he would have more time to think and dwell on the mistakes he had made.

The old man burst out laughing. "You want to imprison me, abi? Do you want to use your power? Alright, I will go. It's just a matter of time before the promised one comes and dethrones you."
Even though he was not a man who typically showed fear, on hearing those words, the Baale shivered.

3

BOLUWATIFE AND ADUNNI FLEE

In Ibadan, there was a man named Boluwatife. He was a hunter who was loved by his family and respected by all. He was married to the love of his life, Adunni. Adunni was a very beautiful girl, simple and sweet. She would never start an argument but would always end any arguments that may arise. Adunni was very diplomatic; she chose her words very carefully. However, if one were wrong, she would waste no time telling the person so. To her, it was preferable for someone to be hurt for just a while, because of an area in their life that needed improvement, rather than for the person to think they were right when they were not, and thereby persist in bad behaviour. That was the kind of person Adunni was.

Adunni was on her way to her mother-in-law's farm when she met an old man. As she was walking by, she greeted the man. "Good morning

Baba." The old man replied: "My child, good morning. How are your parents? I hope they are fine? And your husband, Boluwatife? Hope he is treating you right?"

Adunni replied, "Everything is fine, Baba." As she was walking away, the old man called her back. "Adunni! Come, I almost forgot what I was meant to tell you. Old age, you see, it gets to you. Please, a word of warning: do not let anyone know about your pregnancy. If it is possible, go to another village to have the baby."

Adunni was shocked. She wondered how the old man knew of her pregnancy since she was not visibly showing any signs of being pregnant. She asked the old man a few questions. "Baba, who are you? And how did you know I was with child when I have not even started to show?   I have not even told my husband!"
The old man smiled and replied, "It does not matter who I am, or how I know you're with child, all that matters is that you listen to me and heed my words. Or do you have any brilliant ideas about how to remedy your situation?" He asked sarcastically.

Adunni replied "No, Baba. I'm listening."

The old man replied, "We have passed the stage of how I know about the pregnancy. We are now at the stage of how we will save this child that is in you."

"Save?" Adunni muttered.

"Old one, you talk in riddles, and I am but a child. Why will we need to save a child that has not even been born?"

The man smiled. It was a warm smile, full of kindness and knowledge. Adunni was a well brought up girl indeed.

"Yes, you are pregnant, and not only are you pregnant, but you are carrying a very special child. A child that will start a sequence of events that will span not only this dimension but six others. This child has the power to make or mar the destinies of billions of people."

Adunni dropped the basket that was in her hand and asked the old man, "Are you saying that the child in my womb is the saviour of many?"

The old man laughed. "Why does that shock you? Do you think that Aseda does not know what he is doing? My child, he does. I think they sometimes play games with us humans, wanting to see just how much we can take before we break, but that is a story for another time."

He smiled gently as Adunni stood there, looking shocked. He said to himself, *Obatala messed things up. He should stop drinking, really, what was he thinking? Now we have to try very hard to clean up this stupid mess.*
"Once again back to the matter. As I was saying, make sure no one knows about your pregnancy. If possible, leave this village as soon as you can."

Still feeling very confused, Adunni asked: "Leave? To where? Baba where should I tell my parents that I am going to?"
"Just tell them that you have a trip to make, something about your 'tie and dye' clothes, since that is what you sell for a living", replied the old man. "Please let me not keep you, you have somewhere to go, and I too have some other places to go this morning. Just remember, do not let anyone know about the pregnancy, and all will be well."

The old man left Adunni even more puzzled than he had met her, and the thoughts were racing in Adunni's mind as he went on his way.

Adunni continued with her trip, worried and confused about all that the old man had said to her. She wondered who this man was, that he knew so much about her. He was not a friend to her father nor was he a member of her mother's family, so who was he? How had he known about a pregnancy that she had not told anyone about? Was he trying to help her or put her in harm's way? All these thoughts ran through her mind as she completed all her errands and got home soon, her conversation with the old man still occupied her mind.

Adunni thought about the encounter with the old man all day, and she was so lost in thought that Boluwatife had to ask her what the matter was.

"My love, why are you worried? What could be lying so heavily on your mind that you did not even notice that I am here?"

Adunni sighed heavily and said, "My husband, something happened today that I have never experienced before."

Concerned, Bolu asked, "what did you experience o, my lovely wife? You and your various stories."

He pulled her close and hugged her, his brow furrowed with concern.

Adunni related the events of that afternoon; how she was coming home from her mother-in-law's farm, and she met an old man who told her a very amazing thing.

"My husband, the most amazing thing was that he knew I was pregnant-"

"Hold on," he interrupted, "You're pregnant?" He asked, joy evident in his voice.

"And how did this old man know you were pregnant before I did?"

"That's exactly my point, my husband", Adunni replied. "And he told me that this pregnancy must not be noticed in this village. He said that we must leave this village.

"My husband, the funny part of this whole issue is that I had a dream that I must not stay in this village with this pregnancy. This old man just confirmed what my dream was telling me. Now I want to leave this place."

Bolu was deep in thought for a while, and then he sighed. "Okay, I hear you, but where do you want us to go? How far can we run? How do we even know what we are running from, and when do we stop running?"

She kept silent, so he got up and moved to the other side of the bed to think about what needs to be done. Bolu thought about where they would go all through the night. As the sun rose high in the sky, while working on the farm, the idea of where they would go came to Bolu. As soon as he had the inspiration, he started thinking and working towards it. That evening, while they were having their evening meal, Bolu told his wife.

"Adunni, we will be leaving this village soon, so start getting ready."

Adunni was happy to hear what her husband said. It was one of the reasons she loved him so much; he would always hear her out and consider her feelings, rather than trying to impose his will on her. When she responded to him, it was with relief and a surge of happiness in her voice.

"Yes, my husband! Thank you for listening to me." She exclaimed. "But my husband, where are we going?"

"We are going to settle down in Ilaro."

Two days before they left Ibadan, Adunni and Bolu visited Adunni parents to say goodbye to them. When asked where they were going, they were told that Adunni had been made an offer to come and sell Adire to the royal families of some of the great towns in the land.

Their parents were happy to hear that, but they couldn't understand why the royal families did not send people to choose for them instead of requesting for Bolu and Adunni to bring the fabrics by themselves. Boluwatife told them that the royal families did not want to be seen wearing the same Adire as the commoners and that some of them were going to specify the designs Adunni would make for them.

Boluwatife's father scratched his beard, eyes crinkled in suspicion.
"My son, it's not like I am not happy about this new development, because I am, but I can't help but wonder if you are telling me the whole truth."

Adunni and Bolu looked at themselves nervously, wondering what they should tell the old man.

"Baa mi, I don't understand what you are talking about. Why would we lie to you? I swear to you that the only reason we are leaving the village is because of your daughter's work, and I assure you that we will be back in under a year."

On the day that they were to leave, Adunni had mixed feelings. She felt in her heart that she had to leave the village, but she also felt bad because she was going to miss her family, her friends, and everyone she knew. She consoled herself with the thought that she had to leave the village and her family all in order to save them and billions of others. She could not quite explain it, but she knew in her heart that it was the right thing to do. With heavy and uncertain hearts, Adunni and Boluwatife left their village, weighed down by memories of all the good times they had.

4

AGBEDEMEJI AYE ORUN

[between heaven and earth]

(Nine Years Later)

Malika was standing, and Nimi was floating, backing him. They turned around slowly to face one another and adopted fighting stances. Malika said, "Your combat test is in five days. On your guard, little girl."

Nimi raised her head, staring at the sky through the open roof of the training ground. *Orirun* had been created as a haven for special ones. Although *Agbedemeji Aye* was large and twice as big as *Aye*, *Orirun* was created from the solid mist and situated at the center of *Agbedemeji*. The gates of Orirun glimmered; they could be mistaken for golden glass. *Aseda* had done a beautiful job on the place.

The lands of *Orirun* were made of gold. They shone, and the children could see their reflections on the floor. Anyone who passed through the gate without an exeat would freeze, till Malika came to the gate. Malik was the principal, as well as Nimi's trainer. Some said he was the strongest and wisest of all the *Angelis* both in *Orirun* and *Orun*.

"I'm not that little girl anymore!" With those words, Nimi rose higher, so she was almost at eye level with her trainer. That was how she moved around.

Malika smiled and took a more comfortable stance to defend himself. He was tall - about seven feet, with dark, leathery wings that spanned nine feet. His wings glittered in the fading sun, showing the glory. He had a full head of coarse dark hair. His round, beautiful face and straight, pointed nose would make one almost mistake him for female, but his well-built body and broad shoulders were a testament to the warrior he was. He looked like someone in his mid-twenties, but no one knew for sure. There was a rumour going around *Orirun*; it was said that he was the third creation of *Aseda*. He was always looking young, as such, no one could say how long he had been around.

"I didn't know; you need to remind me of your age."

He sighted her hands reaching for the darts she always kept on her person, and moved swiftly towards her, dodging from side to side as she threw them at him. *Same Nimi, always predictable*, he thought, as he sidestepped the last dart and ducked, grabbing her legs from behind her. He dragged her feet under him, held her legs, and tried to hit her a few inches below her shoulder blades. Nimi dodged the move swiftly, floated higher up, and elbowed him in the chin, which made him loosen his grip on her.

She floated to the other side of the room and hung there, anticipating his next attack. He got up and flew towards her, but she was better prepared. He tried to catch her again, but she swerved and slipped through his hands. Malika then used gravity against her by flying above her and making himself invisible, grabbing her from behind and slamming her on the ground. That hurt Nimi more than she expected. When he saw how she landed, he relaxed. The next series of moves he had planned for her would be unnecessary if she still did not know how to land with coordination when she had been thrown. Straightening to a standing position in mid-air, Malika made a hand signal. An attendant in a corner of the arena sounded the gong, marking the end of the training session for that day.

He leaned over her and said: "Always keep your guard up. Don't be overconfident in battle. Don't rush blindly to attack with everything you've got. Always hold back a bit so you can think of a defence. It could mean you are losing your head or another part of your body. And yes, you are not that little girl anymore, you are older, but I am still your trainer, and you need to listen to me," he called at Nimi as she struggled to sit up and levitated far away from him.

As he walked away, he said to her: "We are done here. From now on, you practice on your own." Nimi was angry, feeling defeated. "How did he do that?" She grumbled as she moved away from him.

Malika dusted his clothes as though there was dirt on them. Although there wasn't any, it was his habit always to dust his clothes after every training session. Nimi left the training arena and was on her way to meet her two best friends and greatest allies: Omitoni and Omoyeni, the divas in her life.

She was received by her friends in the common hall of their hostel. They all called it 'agbala'. The room was magical; it expanded to accommodate the akada (students) in it. When the akadas were few, the room would shrink to hold the fewer number of students.

"How many minutes did you last?" Omoyeni said, stroking Nimi's hair.

"I bet she didn't last up to iseju mewa (ten minutes)," *Omitoni* said jokingly.

"If I strike you with this anger I am feeling ehn, you will be sorry," said Nimi, as she left for her room.

Omoyeni spoke to Omitoni about how she addressed the issue.

"Toni, you need to be more sensitive to Nimi's feelings about Malika defeating her. You know that she hates losing."

Toni shrugged her shoulders and scoffed. "She needs to grow a thicker skin if she is the promised one that everyone is waiting for. She will face some very evil spirits in human bodies and some of these spirits will do some pretty bad jobs on her."

Birds of a feather flocking together was how some people described the relationship between Omoyeni, Omitoni, and Nimi. While the trio may have had similar personalities, in appearance, they were on different sides of the pole.

Omitoni was a dark-skinned, slim lady, about five feet nine inches, and there was a general misconception about the people from her side. It was believed they were always fair-skinned and their skin colour was a gift by the queen who ruled the sea. Omitoni's hair was red, and complimented her brown eyes. Her elegance, poise, and confidence would easily make one mistake her for a princess. In reality, she belonged to a long line of kingmakers, which gave her exclusive rights and conferred some privileges to her, such as attending the school where she was now.

Hours after the conversation, everyone else was asleep. Everyone, except Nimi. She turned restlessly over and over, trying to get a more comfortable position to sleep, but to no avail. Flashes of images ran through her head. She got up from the *ibusun* (bed) and headed to the fountain to drink water. Each room had its fountain that ran from *Orun* to *Orirun* *(heaven to midheaven)*. She drank and returned to her bed, but the images would not let her sleep. She remembered the scene like it was yesterday - she hadn't meant to hurt him. It was just self-defence. Egbetani, the first teacher of Ijakadi she met.

5

THE INCIDENT AT TRAINING

A year and a half previously, Nimi and Egbetani, the Ijakadi instructor had had a clash in the training room. Stretching his wings to sweep her away, she lost concentration and fell to the ground. He grabbed her hand, lifted her, and threw her to the ground. Nimi landed badly and rolled, wincing. She was better at Ijakadi than this. She shook her head to clear it and tried to sit up, but Egbetani descended on her and slammed her to the ground as she tried to sit up. Nimi screamed for help, tears springing to her eyes, but the room was sound-proof and no one could hear her. He landed on her and knelt down, pinning her body under his much larger one. His wings spread out above his back, blocking the light. She looked left and right, looking for help. The attendant who was supposed to be in the room and would ring the gong to signal the end of training had gone out, presumably sent on an errand by Egbetani.

She had heard rumours among the students of how Egbetani overpowered and defiled young girls, but nothing had been proven. She tried to scream again, but Egbetani's hand clamped over her mouth, cutting off her cries for help. She looked around, not liking the look in Egbetani's eyes, but there was no one to help her. She tried to scream again, struggled, and got her left hand free to push him away. Instead of pushing him away, to her shock, lightning came out of her hand to strike him. There was a strange noise, and the acrid smell of burning flesh. Egbetani grunted as the shock tore through him. His wings were charred, and the teacher was thrown off her and fell to the ground. His scream tore through the serene atmosphere of Agbedemeji.

Malik stormed into the arena. "Nimi, by everything holy, if you have done something wrong this time, you will faceeeeeeee........."

He had not finished this statement when he sighted the figure struggling weakly on the floor, torn, blackened wings still smoking. "Nimi..." He asked with shock in his voice, "What in the name of everything holy did you do?"

"I didn't do anything. I swear by Aseda, I didn't do anything." Nimi replied, trembling.
"Wow! I'm wondering if I was the one that touched him then." Malik said sarcastically.

Malik then asked: "what happened?"
"All I know is that he was struck by lightning all of a sudden!" She said in total shock.
"All of a sudden?? What do you mean by all of a sudden? What were you guys doing that could result in him being singed?
For once, Malika wasn't the fiery warrior he was known for being. He seemed to diminish, to become less threatening. Even his wings folded up and tucked themselves in behind him, making the fallen angel look somewhat smaller, if such a thing was possible. He held her by the shoulder and gently pulled her close. "Nimi, what aren't you telling me? You need to tell me what happened," he said very calmly, so as not to unsettle her further.

So Nimi told him of how Egbetani was trying to force himself on her.

Still in shock, Malika responded very calmly: "So you're telling me that you have heard *Egbetani* has been defiling young girls, and that he tried to do the same to you, so you struck him with lighting by mistake and almost killed him?"

Nimi nodded and said yes.

Wonderful, said Malik. "What will I tell Iya Ewe? Alright, go to your room. Training has ended for today. I will handle it."

In Malik's mind, he thought, *Iya Ewe* must have known about *Egbetani,* but she decided to watch what would happen.

Later that day, Malika was sitting in one of the most beautiful rooms in the whole of *Orirun*. The room was fairly big, not the size of the great hall or the dinner chamber, but everything within it was bright and shining the colour of gold. The windows were like the clouds of the sky, floating around, here one minute and there the next. The room contained only two chairs in the centre that faced each other. It was the room used for private and sensitive discussions with Iya Ewe.

Malika was sitting in one chair, his huge wings folded and tucked into the back of the chair. It went without saying that this was a magical chair, it adjusted and fit itself to support the weight and body type of whoever sat in it. When the smaller students sat in it, it moulded itself to fit their tender bodies, now, when the towering Malik sat in it, it had adjusted itself to fit his bulky frame, supporting his wings and back.

Across from Malik, in a throne sat Iya Ewe.

Everyone had ideas and opinions about what *Eledumare* looked like. For the special students at *Orirun, Eledumare* appeared as Iya Ewe, who was a motherly figure and listened to all their worries about life. She was warm and loving, yet very strict. She would often engage in long talks with the students, trying to understand things from their perspective.

Malika asked Iya Ewe, "Would you mind explaining to me- although you don't have to, I would appreciate it- why would you want a nine-year-old girl, who is, even at her best, defenceless, to face a monster like Egbetani? What was your thought process?"

"Well," replied Iya Ewe, "I wanted to see how powerful she was. I mean, Obatala made her, and in his drunken state, he combined the inborn power of four different deities. So I needed to check."

"Let me get this straight", said Malika. "You put her before that monster because you wanted to remember how much power you put in her? Is that what you're telling me?"

"Well," replied Iya Ewe, "When you put it like that, it does sound heartless. I don't think I thought it through. Maybe I was wrong, but I knew she would be able to defend herself, either consciously or instinctively, subconsciously. She does not know the full extent of her power, and it is better tested here than down on Aye."

Malika had to agree with Iya Ewe that it was indeed better for Nimi's powers to be tested here in Orirun than she hurt someone mistakenly in Aye.

What do you have in mind for Egbetani? Malika asked Iya Ewe.

Clearly, he can't still be a teacher here anymore, and Orun is not even a place for him, so…

Her voice changed a little and the room shook as she boomed: *"let it be decreed that the Angel Egbetani is banished from both heaven and earth, he shall remain in purgatory as a wanderer without destination or home."*

*   *   *   *
*

Nimi gulped water and was jolted back to life by *Oketinlegun,*

"I thought you were one of the *Alijanu* banned from *Orirun,* with the way you stood", *Oketinlegun* said.

Many doubted that a boy like *Oke* would be part of the *Iginle* group, with the way he behaved, but Malika knew best. Like *Nimi, Oke* floated two inches off the ground but the difference between the two was that while Nimi floated all the time, *Oke* floated sometimes. This made all the other Iginle members wonder why he wasn't in the *Ebun* group, but Malik knew why he put him there.

"Oke! Se ara e ya? Are you alright in the head? Why would you try to scare me like that?"

Nimi was feeling very cautious ever since the incident with Egbetade. Malika had advised her not to mention it to anyone, but she was wary of her powers running out of control if she got scared or startled.

"Me?! Scare you? How can that happen? Aren't you Nimi, the great warrior? Fear should not exist for someone like you," he said, a naughty smile on his face.

"Funny. So because I am a warrior, as you say, I shouldn't have fear or be afraid when I feel threatened? Is that what you are telling me?" asked Nimi, irritated.

With a mischievous smile on his face, Oke shrugged his shoulders and said: "Well, it is easy for one to think that way, with the way everyone in this school talks about you, from the teachers to the students."

There were four groups of *Akadas* at *Orirun*.
The *Iginles*:
These were unable to use their lower limbs. They were easily identified by their levitation and by their wrist bands - their wisdom was

unquantifiable, though they spent most of their time alone and do not try to socialize. They are compensated for their poor social skills by being very good at critical thinking and problem-solving. Nimi belonged to this group

Adunayes:
These were very jovial, unlike the *Iginles*. Typically the life of the party and joy to the world. Smiles were always plastered on their faces, and they never got angry. They excelled at arts and crafts. The walls of *Orirun* were designed by them. Their flowered headbands were not the only thing that made them distinct; they also had a certain aura around them. It was as though one could become excited just by being near them.

Irawos.
These sets of *Akandas* were either deaf or dumb. Some were both, but they had telepathic powers and could project their thoughts into other people's minds. It was said that this group had the most powerful individuals; that was before Nimi came and changed the order of things in the school. As expected, this did not sit well with them.

Ebuns:

Similarly to the Iginles, most of these were unable to use their lower limbs, although some could. Because of this, some of them who were paralysed from the waist down could levitate. They had various abilities that made them unique. They were intelligent, could teleport from one spot to another, and, much like the Iginles, could control some aspects of the weather. They were also good at manipulation, much like the Iginles.

6

THE BORING WEEKEND

Usually during the weekends, there were no classes, trips, or assignments. Nimi and her friends were typically bored during the weekends. On one of such weekends, the girls got an idea that set Nimi on the path of her destiny.

"Omoyeni, I am bored. In fact, we are all bored. What do you suggest we do this weekend?" asked Nimi.

Omitoni rolled around a little in the waterfall in the back of their room for a second and then with a gleam in her eyes, she said: "Girls! I have a great idea."

Omoyeni rolled her eyes and said: "I hope this idea will not get either me or Nimi in trouble o because I can't afford for another bad report to reach my parents this time. On second thought, today is so boring, what is your idea?" Omoyeni said, a mischievous smile playing on her face.

"I trust you do not want to be left out," Omitoni said.
"Well, my idea is this: why don't we go to Aye and see what the teachers are always talking about?"

Nimi and Omoyeni slowly turned around, forgetting the fact that they were swimming, and asked Omitoni in unison: "ARE YOU MAD???"

Omitoni jumped up, and asked: "What? Aren't you the least bit curious about Aye? Don't you want to know how truly messed up Aye is for us to be trained this much, that Omoyeni has to take water time just to be able to catch up with training? Nimi, you are looking at me like that, but you never even bothered to ask Malik why you were being trained, and every time you're coming in from training looking like someone who fought with an elephant."

"Well, he always said it had to do with my destiny, so I got tired and stopped asking. I assumed that, when it was time, I would be told, or shown."

Trust Nimi to not let something as important as why it was her responsibility to save Aye go.

By and by, as they discussed, Omitoni convinced all of them that it was a good idea to go to Aye. They thought about how to leave Orirun. "Let's teleport down to Aye."

"Wait, I know we normally use our teleporting powers in class when we are being trained. What if we make a mistake in going from one place to another?" Omitoni said with concern.

Omoyeni replied, who told you that we will use our powers separately? I have no plans to be cut in half, thank you very much. Nimi is easily the best student in the class, we will use Nimi's teleporting skills.

Nimi and Omitoni thought that was a great idea, so they also agreed.

In Nimi's eyes, you could see the mix of emotions when she saw Aye for the first time. It was unclear which emotion was greater: the excitement of seeing a new place or the fear of the unknown. She saw people walking with their legs and wondered how that felt. To avoid looking strange, she and her friends decided that she would be carried by Omoyeni. It would be strange to see a young girl floating two inches off the ground. They went straight to the centre of the village, to the marketplace where they saw wonderful things. They couldn't stay for long because they knew that Malika would soon be looking for the three of them.

They had just gotten back to Atunida when they heard that Malika was looking for Nimi, because she needed to commence the last stage of her training.

"Nimi! Where have you been? I have been looking for you all over the place!" yelled Malika.

Right after the training, Nimi and her friends returned to Aye.

On their second visit, Nimi and her friends went back to the same place they had been to the first time. It was while they were there that they heard about the wicked and tyrannical Baale that had been making mothers live without their children. They overheard some villagers talking.

"Did you hear that another baby was left at the riverside?"

"I heard o, my sister!"

"Why is this Baale so afraid of these children that are different sef? Why kill them?"

My sister, there is a saying that goes "we fear only what we don't understand"

"If he knows that they don't get killed but that they are taken away, there will be trouble o!"

"Are you telling me? Don't you remember the last mother that tried to defy him was killed alongside her baby and her whole family? That was a really sad day."

Nimi, Omitoni and Omoyeni were shocked by the words they overheard.

"Now you can see why I wanted us to come to Aye," said Omoyeni.

"These people suffer a lot Nimi, and you were chosen to save them."

They had to go back to Orirun because the very next day was the final test for all the students in Nimi's set.

7

COMBAT!

On the day of combat, all the students there were very anxious about the test. Each student's trainer was present.

When it got to Nimi's turn, Malik came to the centre of the training mat and asked her if she was ready. He had tried to make sure it was a level playing field for both of them. "Remember all I have taught you," he said before the fight began.

The *Iginle* passed the group event, thanks to Nimi who saw a window of opportunity and took it. While fighting, she noticed that Malik had become distracted by something, or someone, and he wasn't paying full attention to the fight. When he should have blocked her attack, he was careless and so she got a chance to defeat him. Malika was a bit disappointed in himself because he was not paying attention to what he was doing, but he accepted it and acknowledged them as winners.

Nimi wanted to know the reason why Malik was so distracted. While everyone was celebrating her and her friends, she noticed that Malik had left the fighting arena. Wondering where he was going, she called her friends Omoyeni and Omitoni and they followed, wanting to know where he was going. they could barely contain their shock when they saw him leaving Orirun.

Omitoni asked: "where is he going?"
Nimi replied: "Are you asking me? How am I to know where he is going? Should we go and ask him where he is going?"
Omitoni murmured, "There is no need for that na.

Still following him, their shock increased when they realized that he went to the same village they had visited the last two times they were in Aye. They decided to follow him and see what he would do.

Malika went to the riverside, after reaching Aye via the portal by the road path to the forest and that was when they realized that it was the same river that the villagers had been talking about.

From their hiding place, they saw him emerge and summon Aja, who appeared from the bushes, his fur thick and shaggy, and his teeth looking as sharp as knives. His eyes glowed, as yellow as ever.

"My old friend, you are here!" said the dog. "It's been quite a while since I last saw you, hasn't it? You have been sending someone to me instead. This one you came by yourself, it must be very important."

Malik replied: "Yes. Nine years ago, to be exact."
"And what about the promised one? Hope she is learning?"
"Nimi is learning and causing mischief up and down Orirun."
They both laughed as if it was expected of her.

Nimi, hiding in the bushes with her friends, was shocked to realize that she was one of the children that she heard the villagers talking about. So shocked in fact, that she forgot that she had followed Malik to Aye and that she wasn't alone.

She promptly levitated out and asked in a small voice: "Was this where you found me?"
Shocked, but not quite surprised, Malik murmured, "I know that I just didn't hear what I heard just now. Old friend, please tell me that I am dreaming."

Aja sighed dramatically, shaking his head, and said: "He wants me to lie, and he knows I can't lie to save my life." *"Wo Malika, ma je kin wo oju e o!"* (look, Malik, don't let me get angry with you).

Malik shouted: "Nimi, go back. You are not meant to be here! No one must see you!"
"WHY AM I NOT MEANT TO BE SEEN?" yelled Nimi.

Malika, struggling to be calm, replied: "It is not yet the time appointed for you to introduce yourself to the world. And your training is incomplete... You are not ready!"
"Who told you that I am not ready?" replied Nimi, anger in her eyes as she hovered, gliding back and forth along the riverbank.
"The way you are acting is a clear sign that you are not ready", replied Malika.

8

THE DISCOVERY

What started as a joke was fast becoming more than she bargained for. From leaving Orirun to visit this village, to the things she heard about the Baale. However, Malika was the last person she expected to see here. What in the world was he doing here? She chuckled to herself quietly as she realized that asking what *she* was doing here would be the more appropriate question. She had wandered away from her friends to discover this small river situated in nowhere.

She was not the only one who was surprised. Malika was here also, and he was stunned. He knew she would probably be breaking rules by leaving school, given her antecedents and all the mischiefs she and her friends got up to at Atunida, but he had never thought he would see her at that particular place and time. Looking at Nimi, Malika remembered the day he picked her up by the riverside. Seeing the mark on her arm and realizing that she was who he had been waiting for - the past, present, and future, all together in one.

You are not ready, Malika had said to her

Nimi was not ready to leave without an explanation, she had heard right that she was the one being referred to. Malika had kept this secret from her for too long and she felt the right time for the discussion had come.

"I am not leaving without an explanation", she replied, her brow furrowed, arms folded.

The darkness was giving way already, the sun was fast rising, the first cock had crowed 'Kukurukuuuu'. It was dawn already, the river was beginning to sparkle in the dawn. This meant that people would soon come to fetch water for cooking and washing. She knew Malika was right, it was time to leave.

She relented.

"I will leave, but this is not over. We will have this discussion as soon as we get to Agbedemeji", she said with all the confidence she could muster. She could not guess what Malika was thinking from his inscrutable face, and a tiny nod was the only sign he gave that he had even heard her.

Malika turned his back, and spread his wings. A portal, glowing with flashes of lightning, opened ahead of him. This was the first time Nimi would be seeing them stretched out in full. He walked through the portal, and the portal disappeared as he vanished.

A few weeks ago, she had made a promise to herself to be as courteous as she could to everyone, but here she was, talking back at the principal of her school who doubled as her adopted father.

She joined Omotoni and Omoyeni a few feet away from the riverside. The trip to Agbedemeji seemed like forever, as all she thought about was the encounter she had with Malika.

She had explained everything that happened to Omitoni and Omoyeni. They did not know what to say, and kept quiet throughout the trip. The relationship between Nimi and Malika was complicated, to say the least.

There was no need to be sneaky about entering school again, they reasoned, as they entered the school grounds, no longer worried about being caught. Their problems had been traded for much bigger ones. As they approached their rooms, Omitoni broke the silence.

"So Malika was the saviour of all those children that the Baale wanted dead! I am shocked, to say the least. To imagine that in a village, children are feared instead of being loved is so sad."

"So, Nimi, where did you come from, then? Omoyeni asked, her curiosity showing on her face.

Nimi had it in mind to ask Malika, but she did not think Omoyeni would blurt it out.

"Malika will most likely have an answer", she murmured, as her friends turned down the hallway. She needed answers and Malika was the only one she knew to ask. She hoped he was willing to give her those answers. If not, you would find it easier to get answers from a brick wall than from Malika. She said her goodbyes to her friends and headed towards Malika's office. She was lost in thought as she headed down the corridor, so she did not notice Oketinlegun, the clown of their class.

He decided to tease her as he was fond of.

"I must be really tiny", he said.

His words jolted Nimi from her musings.

Eedua! Where did you come from? Nimi exclaimed.

Oketinglegun chuckled loudly, the crowing of a successful prankster. He had achieved his aim. "You finally see me, that is nice. This one you are lost in thought like this, where are you going?"

"I am headed to the principal's office, how are you doing?" Nimi murmured distractedly.

"I'm doing good, I wonder what you have done this time", Oketinlegun replied.

Nimi did not bother to reply. She merely kept moving past him and onto her destination, as she was not in the mood to exchange words with him or anyone. He was a bit of a busybody, and she felt his curiosity about her affairs was the last thing she needed.

She was flustered as she knocked on the door of Malaika's office. Her anxiety had her feeling like she was going into a fight situation.

'You can come in', he called from inside.

Nimi went in, saw him sorting through files and folders, and her tongue tied. She closed her eyes and took a deep breath. Now or never…

"Who am I?" asked Nimi.

"Excuse me?" asked Malika, with absolutely no surprise in his eyes.

Nimi glided towards Malika and repeated her question, practically shouting. "Who am I?"

She knew if she backed down now, that might be the end of the matter.

He knew she was angry, but she was sounding rude in her approach, and he was not going to condone any form of rudeness.

"You left the school without permission, broke a lot of rules, intruded into *my* personal life, and now you are screaming at me and raising your voice, asking who you are… That is wrong."

"I've got a question for you. Who do you want to be? A rude, spoilt, and entitled child? Regardless of who you think you are, or what you overheard, which was obviously not meant for your ears, you will not talk to me like that, or disrespect my office in such a manner." Malaika snapped back at her, a hint of irritation showing in his normally level and calm voice.

"I am sorry for all I have put you through. I accept whatever punishment is assigned to me because of my actions, but I plead that my friends not be punished as I was the one who cajoled them into following me." she said apologetically.

Malik looked at Nimi, face devoid of expression, and said: "I will answer your questions, but why do you want to know anyway? The truth brings nothing but sadness at times.

"Well, the reason why I'd like to know where I am from is that the way you are acting is very suspicious. It got me thinking, and so there must be something about me that nobody is telling me."

"What if I tell you that there's nothing wrong? What if I say that you're not that special? Why would you think that you are special? Is it because I'm training you myself, or because I have been giving you the treatments deserving of a warrior?"

Nimi's face fell when she heard his words.

Malika felt bad that he didn't tell Nimi what she wanted to know. However, having trained her, he knew how her mind worked; the probability of her staying in school after knowing that people were suffering and waiting for her was really low. She would want to charge out to go and help whoever needed help at once. Plus, she was nowhere ready to fight that battle. Telling her the truth was not going to do anyone good at this time. Thinking more on this topic, Malika thought it would be best to strip her of her powers, which made him wonder if it could be done. This question was on his mind when he went to see Iya Ewe later that day to ask her a few questions

Malika went to Iya Ewe's audience room and sat down. He had a lot on his mind, and he was pondering how to phrase the question. He jerked a bit as he realized that Iya Ewe had appeared, and he had been staring at Iya Ewe for a while. Usually, Iya Ewe had the most comforting smile; creatures of all kinds always responded positively to her smile, but the weight of the words in his heart tied his tongue, and he found himself struggling to smile back at her. Her smile never faltered, - and then she asked Malika, "Are you going to ask your questions, or should I just answer without hearing the question?"

Malika sighed and looked her straight in the eye. "Can Nimi's powers be stripped from her?

"It depends", she muttered, with a tiny shrug. "Why do we want to strip her of her powers?"

"We need to strip her of her powers in order to keep her safe"

"Why do we need to keep her safe? Is the school compromised? Or," Iya Ewe inclined her head ever so slightly, and asked, "Did she leave the school and go to Aye?

Malika decided not to answer the question. He knew the direction the discussion would take, and he was not prepared for it. So he decided to switch tactics.

"Why, in the name of all that is holy, did you let Obatala drink and give her so much power and bravery, and finish it off with a strong headedness that can't be controlled?"

Iya Ewe's smile shifted a little and she shrugged. "I wasn't there when he moulded her. I was just told that Obatala took it upon himself to fulfil the prophecy. I am merely trying to keep the girl alive."

9

TRAINING COMPLETED

Ten years later

The day started with so much promise of being a great day. Nimi woke up feeling very happy. Getting up from her *ibusun,* she neither complained nor grumbled that she had to get up. Today was a happy day. It was the beginning of the rest of her life. She and her friends had been making plans on how she was going to party all day without anything stopping her joy. Thinking about how she was going to miss Orirun and everything, she became sad. Orirun was the only home she had ever known; her only safe place since she had been a baby left to die by the riverside.

Now that her training had (finally) been completed, she would have to leave, and that made her sad. She was torn between the excitement of seeing a new world on Aye, and the sense of sadness and finality as she was finally leaving the only place she had ever called home. She was torn from her musing as Omoyeni practically danced into the room, quivering with excitement.

"Nimi! You are not ready yet?" Omoyeni called, a little too loudly. What was the point in yelling if the person you were yelling at was right in front of you?

"I just have to wear this ceremonial dress and I will be done"

Omoyeni stared at the cut and style of the ceremonial attire. The vibrant colours of the cloth complimented Nimi's skin tone, making it stand out more.

"Erm… Nimi, this is a great design. How come you get to wear something different from the ceremonial clothes we have to wear?"

"Omoyeni did you forget so fast?" Omitoni, who had just entered the room asked, pride in her voice. "Today Nimi will take a solemn vow to protect all the defenseless in Aye and to always fight to rid the world of all the evil that exists in it.

Now, Omitoni, I will get to see if the scary tales they told us about Aye are true, and if the evil they say is in the world is as bad as they say it is." replied Nimi

"And we will be right next to you as usual", Omitoni said, with Omoyeni nodding her assent.

Nimi saw the determination and love that they radiated and knew for a fact that they would always be there. This filled her with happiness to know that no matter what happened after now, Omoyeni and Omitoni would always be there, her family, her personal people.

While they were chatting away, the big gong rang, signalling the beginning of the day's activities
"Well, as much as I would love to stay here and chat with you, we have to go. I wouldn't..."

As she was still trying to get the girls out of the *ibusun*, there was a knock at the door. Another knock came some seconds later, and Malika walked in with an obvious smile on his face.
"Is it me, or has the gong been rung?" asked Malika, looking at Omoyeni and Omitoni who had terrified smiles on their faces. The typically taciturn fallen angel never smiled, never showed any expression. The smile of today, plus his height and sheer bulk, got the girls flustered and shy, and Omoyeni and Omitoni hurried out of the room.

Malika turned to Nimi and asked, "Are you ready?"
Nimi replied, "Yes, I am."
"It's been 19 years of watching you grow into the young lady that you are. Competent and loyal, a beacon of hope for the helpless., I thank Aseda for allowing me to be your guide and trainer.
Nimi, I want you to remember that your powers were not given to you just for the sake of it, this power you have is so great, it can make or mar the existence of this world we live in. Also, remember that as the leader of the Undesirables, you have to keep your eyes on the ball at all times. It's easy to lose focus when emotions take over, but always remember to always look at the bigger picture and ignore all those insignificant ones.

Nimi looked at him. she remembered when she was younger, wilder and full of trouble. He_had been calm and understanding, with her, never giving up on her. Although he had been firm when she had been headstrong, she knew it was for her own good. "Thank you Oluko, I will put that in mind." Malika looked at her, blinked, and said "We need to go, the celebration is about to start."

As they got there, they saw that all the set of *akadas* that had completed their training were already settled and waiting quietly in their seats. This was unusual for the typically unruly bunch.

Malika was somewhat surprised to see them seated. "Do they want to leave that bad?" He murmured.

"One would think that you were not happy to see us go." Nimi replied, amusement in her voice. "Mind you, not all of us are going to Aye, some of us decided that they won't leave this place. Which reminds me, honest question, "what is wrong with Oketinlegun? why won't he go home?"

"Soon, all will be revealed", replied Malika. "Give it some time, and you will know everything. In the meantime, let me go and deliver my speech."

Malika got up and moved to the front of the Akada, looking at their eager, solemn faces, and letting the memories wash over him, names and faces and places, remembering how each and every student got to the school.

Akada, Today is the beginning of a new era for all of you. For the past 19 years, you have been trained, taught… And shown how to do things the right way, many of you were brought here from various other places, dimensions, and worlds. As

Malika said these words, all the Akada were shocked. They probably had no idea that not all of them were human.

Omoyeni leaned toward Nimi and asked, "Were you aware?"

Nimi stared at Omoyeni from the corner of her eye. She didn't dare turn towards Omoyeni. After all, they were sitting on the first row and Malika was looking right at her daring her to say a word.

"Aware of what exactly? The fact that there were other dimensions or that we were going to school with other undesirable from other dimensions? Which question are you asking?" mumbled Nimi from the corner of her mouth.

"Both, I guess", muttered Omoyeni.

"Well, the answer to your question is no. I was not aware that we were going to school with undesirables from other dimensions"
Malika was clearing his throat to get them to stop talking. The girls sat up and paid attention.

"You all have been trained to be a lasting solution in your various worlds. Here in school, you were put in groups to help your teachers strengthen your core gifts and talents, and to also show you that you are not alone, that there are others like you. You were taught acceptance, courage, unity, and a sense of right from wrong. Some of you have made lasting friends from this school and some forever enemies." He fixed Nimi with a knowing look.

This made Nimi uncomfortable and worried about everything. She unconsciously wandered down memory lane. From when her training started at the age of five to her encounter with the paedophilic fallen angel (who, she had heard, was still angry about losing his wings) to her brief encounter in 2nd year at *Orirun*. She hoped that Egbetade would one day find peace and the help he badly needed. She was lost in thought when Omoyeni jabbed her sharply. She jerked, startled, just in time to hear the last bits of Malika's speech: "… and now without further delay, let's hear what the top student for this year has to say"

Ayanfeoluwanimi (I am God's chosen one) please come forward.

On hearing her name, Nimi got up and hovered towards the stage. Her mind was in a number of places, but she took a deep breath to steady herself. She positioned herself right at the centre and cleared her throat.

She stood, looking at the sea of faces. Imagining herself staring each graduate student right in the eye.

I can do this, she thought.

Nimi raised her hands high and yelled, "My fellow akadas. We finally made it!

The gathered students clapped politely.

Malika shook his head and murmured to himself. This Nimi girl would never change. So predictable, and yet he found himself smiling as she continued.

"It's been nineteen years, my fellow akadas. Nineteen years of training, learning, understanding who we are, and of course what we can do, with our various talents. For some of us, it has been fun all the way; for others a hard time they would love to forget, but for the likes of me and my friends, it has been an adventure, an adventure that we dearly wish we could go on, again and again."

As she said this, some of the hitherto blank faces began to smile. Nearly all the akadas had fond memories of the things they had seen, done, and encountered in the course of their stay.

Nimi allowed herself a brief smile, and then she continued.

"All in all, we have learned to help, save and protect those weaker than us. Our abilities make us different and the majority of those living in Aye will not understand us. All that they will see is that we are not like them, and they will wonder why. Some of them may be unfriendly, because people will always fear what they don't understand. That's alright, as long as we know who we are, the undesirables know how to look at the big picture.

Nimi looked at all the *Akada* in attendance one by one, with a smile, and then she asked "Can all the *aseyori* please rise up?" Six students floated in midair, grinning from ear to ear, proud of who or what they were.

Nimi looked at them and nodded. Then she turned to the principal and said "Sir, we are ready to help keep Aye balanced."

Then they all knelt before Malika in respect to his tutelage.

Malika looked at all seven of them with pride and joy in his heart, remembering where and how he came across each one of them. Almost tearing up,

he cleared his throat and said "Aseda be with you and guide you"
They all replied in unison "ASE!"

10

DEALING WITH THE TRUTH

As the party was going on, Malika grew more anxious and worried as the hour went by. His anxiety was caused by the fact that they had to finally tell Nimi the truth, and he wasn't so sure that Nimi could handle what the truth was. In fact, considering her nature, she just might walk out of Orirun without hesitation. This character of hers was the major reason why he didn't tell her who she was when she had first asked, nine and a half years ago. And why he had never told her, all the times she had asked after then. But now the unavoidable time had come, when he would have to bring her up to speed on who she was and why she mattered so much.

"Where is that blessed four-legged partner of mine when I need him?" Malika muttered under his breath.

"Were you looking for me?" asked Aja, coming around the corner with an innocent smile on his face.

"Yes, I was looking for you", replied Malika. "Where were you?"

"Oh, I was around, looking at things, watching the kids, and amazed at how much they have grown."

"Well, it's time."

Aja decided to play dumb a little, knowing fully well that Malika wasn't in a particularly great mood.

"Time for what? Has another child been dropped? Can't we have even today free?"

"Who is talking about going to pick up another child! See, don't get on my last nerve today o. Were we not meant to tell Nimi everything about her life today?"

"Oh! I forgot. Thank God I hadn't left, saw a wonderful-looking meaty piece of bone in Aye while I was listening to Nimi give her speech, and I was dreaming of how best to eat it, but now that you have mentioned this, then I guess we, or rather I, will have to wait for a short/long while. Hopefully, I can still get to eat the bone later", Aja mumbled.

"Aja, can you be serious for once?" asked Malika.

"Well, I am not too sure I am capable of actually being serious but let's see what happens.

Malika looked down wondering why Iya Ewe had decided to make Aja his partner because he just could not believe the carefree attitude that this dog, bigger than him himself, was always presenting. If not that he knew for certain that the dog was a spirit being he would have wondered where Iya Ewe got him from.

Malika was more worried about Nimi and how she would take the news that she was to be the leader of the undesirables. It would definitely be a shock to tell her the truth, prophecy and all. Knowing her character, he was hoping that she would be able to cope with everything he was about to tell her. Nimi liked to run from responsibility, but who knew?

Malika looked across the room and watched Nimi laughing with the other six *aseyori* and he dreaded telling her everything.

How was he meant to tell her that because a man feared the fact that a certain child would exist, he ordered the death of all malformed children. This news needs a soft landing, he mused.

"Aja where is Imoran?"

Aja looked confused for a moment then he remembered "Oh! Imoran!. Your little present for Nimi is waiting outside, I was wondering why you would ask me to bring Imoran here for Nimi. I thought they were not meant to meet till later on, when she goes into an actual battle."

"Well, I changed my mind", replied Malika. "If everything goes as planned then he will return home with you, but if not… then he may have to go with Nimi."

"You are still worried about Nimi's reaction to the truth aren't you?" asked Aja

"Absolutely!" replied Malika. "She is very defiant at her best then add into the mix that she is not really like the other undesirables; won't you be worried too? I tell you, Aja for the past five months I haven't…"

"Wait!" Aja stopped him in midsentence. "What do you mean by in five months you haven't? You haven't what, slept or eaten? I honestly don't understand what you are talking about o. See eh don't worry about Nimi she will be fine. "

Malika took a deep breath. "Let's hope so."

He turned to where Nimi was chatting with her friends and called her.

"Nimi! A moment of your time, please"

Nimi turned towards Malika and signalled that she was coming. She then turned to Omitoni and Omoyeni and said something to them.

She turned around and saw that Malika and his four-legged partner were walking towards Malika's office so she followed them.

"I wonder what they want to tell me now", she mused.

"Maybe they want to tell you who you really are", replied Oketinlegun, who was standing by. "And how would you know that?" asked Nimi.

"Well, I think that the fact that they are moving the meeting place to somewhere private may be a sign of the kind of talk they want to have with you."

Then Oketinlegun rolled his eyes and said, "What do I even know? I am just an eighteen-year-old boy who has no idea about anything."

Nimi said, "Honestly, I don't know how you know things that you know."

"Reading your mind and their minds", he replied with a smile.

Nimi hurried down to Malika's office, when she got there she knocked on the door with confidence.

Enter! called Malika. As Nimi entered the room, she immediately saw that Malika was not alone, she saw two dogs, one looking very familiar and another one that she had never seen before. This made her wonder what he needed to talk to her about. "You summoned me, Oluko."

"Yes, Nimi, I did, sit down."

"Nice seeing you again Nimi, it's been a while", Aja huffed, his tongue lolling out and making the huge dog look like he was smiling.

"Good afternoon Sir", said Nimi, trying to remember where she had seen this magnificent dog before.

Seeing the confusion on her face, Aja told her, "We met on your last wonderful adventure to Aye which led to your powers being stripped from you. "

Oh! You are his partner! Now I remember! Nice seeing you again."

Malika took a deep breath and repeated himself "Ayanfeoluwanimi sit down"

On hearing her full name being called, Nimi sat down. A cold feeling settled in the pit of her belly.

"The reason I called you here is to reveal a few important things to you about who and what you stand for." On hearing this, Nimi sat straight and paid full attention to the words Malika was saying. She held herself still, willing herself to be calm.

"Centuries ago, a prophecy was told both in Aye and Orun, about 7 heroes who would save not only Aye, but six other dimensions. The prophecy was deep and confusing."

Malika stood up and went to the wall of his office, he placed his palm there, made a quick movement, and a secret panel opened. The fallen angel took out a scroll and walked back to Nimi and handed over the scroll to her.

Nimi took the scroll, willing her hands not to shake. The scroll was old, ancient. She opened the seals carefully. On opening the scroll the words jumped at her:

In the time of tyranny, fear was enthroned.

There was gnashing of teeth and wailing under a cruel and oppressive government

Babies, still covered in blood, are torn from their mothers' arms.

The cries of babies make the river unapproachable.

No one knows what lies there.

No one is brave enough to find out.

Everyone is scared.

Who cares?!

Forever? No, this won't go on forever.

There will be a revolt, led by one of those who cry at the riverbank.
An army will rise, and all will follow their voice.

On reading the scroll, Nimi was surprised and confused. Not knowing what to say, she handed the scroll back to Malika. He collected the scroll and dropped it back on the table.

"Why didn't you ever tell me this?" she asked.

"Because you were not ready to have such dumped on your lap too early in life. You needed the time to grow and learn without the weight of the prophecy hanging on your neck."

"Why did you lie to me when I asked who I was ten years ago?" asked Nimi, tears in her voice.

"Because knowing you the way I do, you would have taken off to try and save Aye and I knew that you were not ready. They would have made short work out of you."

"So now may I ask, do I have parents or am I an orphan?"

"Your parents are alive. Alive but old, and you can never go to them."

Nimi's eyes widened in shock. Malika sat there, face impassive as usual. She looked from him to his partner. It was impossible to tell a facial expression on the face of a dog. She looked around the room, trying to steady herself. It was at this time that she caught sight of Imoran, seated very quietly in the corner.

"Who or what is that? She asked Malika
Turning to where she was pointing Malika replied, "That, my dear young woman, is your graduation gift, your new partner, your companion"
"So in short, my new bodyguard. Here I was thinking that I am now free from you only for you to present me with a bodyguard. Amazing!"
Malika's face remained inscrutable. He might as well have been carved out of marble.
Why do I even need a bodyguard? Nimi asked .
Malika looked at the young woman sitting in front of him and sighed. He had grown fond of her, and he had tried as much as possible to keep her sheltered from the ugliness and evil that was so prevalent in the world. She was brave, almost foolishly so, and yet her time here was up, and she had no idea that her life as she knew it was about to change forever. He was trying to look out for her, and he knew that Imoran would be her pillar of

strength in some of the darkest days and years to come.

"Humour me and accept this my gift. I can't always be with you but Imoran will never leave your side", said Malika. He could see that she was already caving in so he drove home the point.

"Think of him as that very powerful pet that will obey your every word."

Aja laughed; a weird, funny doggy-dog sound that somehow left its meaning undeniable. He knew that this would never happen.

What's so funny? asked Malika in his mind.

Aja and Malika had a telepathic link that they employed when they could not speak openly.

"Oh, nothing", replied Aja, via the same link.

"Okay, fine", replied Nimi. "I know I am not leaving this room unless I accept him anyway." She raised herself from the chair and glided toward Imoran. "So, what is your name of my new bodyguard?"

"My name is Imoran" (advice)

"Imoran, you say?"

Nimi moved forward to touch his head. Just as her fingertips touched his fur, there was a spark and a sizzle, and a dull orange glow that covered both

Nimi and Imoran. As the light faded Nimi wondered to herself what had just happened, and to her surprise she heard Imoran mumble, "I too was wondering" clearly in her mind. A quick look confirmed that the dog was nuzzling her hand, not talking out loud. It was at that moment that they realized that they could communicate telepathically.

Nimi turned to Malika and Aja.

"What just happened? Nimi asked, her voice low, mostly because she was struggling very hard not to scream.

Aja looked down at his huge forepaws, and mumbled, "Did I forget to mention that Imoran is a spirit being?

Malika looked shocked that Imoran was a spirit being.

You this blessed spirit why didn't you lead with that!" asked Malika

I assumed you were aware! You asked me to get Nimi a present and I did. Wait, wait, were you expecting me to get her a normal animal? asked Aja.

"You have a point there" said Malika.

While all this was going on, Nimi looked extremely confused. "Oluko, please what are you trying to tell me?"

"Well", Malika said, "It would seem like you created a telepathic link with Imoran unknowingly"

"What does that mean?" asked Nimi.

"It means that you and Imoran are connected via your mind", Aja replied.

"What!" Nimi shouted, gliding back and forth in the room. "What is this now?"

She stopped, glaring at Malika and his canine partner, who were seated, watching her, and took a deep breath.

"Okay, can it be reversed?

"No it can't."

Malika had his granite face on. One could never quite tell what he was feeling from the tone of his voice or his face.

"That's the funny thing about telepathic connections; it only happens when two beings are meant to be in each other's lives", Aja quipped. "See, let me give you an example: Malika and I have our minds linked to help us with the business of saving abandoned children. Now that's for work, and the only way this link can be broken is maybe if children stop being abandoned by the riverside."

"So you're telling me that this is a 'for life' kind of thing?" asked Nimi.

"Now you get the idea." replied Aja.

At this point Nimi's temper got the better of her.

"Why would you trick me like this? Is it not bad enough that I am separated from my parents, and I will never know who they are? Must I now be linked to a spirit dog for the rest of my life?"

Malika's face did not move a muscle.

"Calm down Nimi", said Aja. "There is no need for you to start shouting like this."

"No need! she said, no need? There is every need to be angry!" shouted Nimi

"Firstly", she ticked off a finger, "I was left for dead, and yes, I know that I am alive now but that does not change the fact that I was left for dead."

"Secondly, I just learnt that I have been chosen to face a Baale who is stark raving mad at best and depending on what happens, I might and the emphasis on **might,** have to kill him.

Now I am linked to a spirit dog! Who knows what will happen next?"

"I can see that this is a lot to deal with, and if I must be honest, we could have handled this whole situation differently." Aja was trying to calm her down. Malika might have been carved from marble; he did not so much as move one of his elegantly sculpted eyebrows.

"Well, you didn't!" shouted Nimi, raging. She wanted to throw something, smash something. Looking round Malika's office, seeing all the training weapons in the room; something occurred to her.

"Why is it that it's only during training that I feel my powers in me?" She asked

"Seriously, Nimi. Don't you think you are about to overstep?" asked Malika.

"I DON'T CARE!!!" shouted Nimi. "Tell me what I want to know!"

Malika stared impassively at her.

"Why can't I use my powers outside of training? Answer me!"

Malika stood up calmly and walked towards Nimi, who was hovering in the air. His steely gaze met hers. "I have constantly told you that there will be no disrespect when you talk to me. Now I would suggest that you calm down, sit down, and let me explain."

On seeing the look in Malika's eyes, Nimi knew that she needed to calm down and listen to what Malika had to say.

"Yes we blocked your powers, and we had to, because when you were young, some accidents happened. To avoid such happening again, we had to block them, not to mention the fact that you could not be controlled made the decision easier."

Nimi got up and glided to where Malika was.

"So what you are telling me is that I needed to be normal to be trained?"

"Nimi, be reasonable. You were young, you were using your power without control. You needed to be subdued to teach you the value of restraint."

Nimi felt betrayed and sad. Sad that the one who was meant to trust her the most took away her powers and left her without help.

11

POWERLESS

Moving from one place to another became more difficult when her powers started getting erratic. She had started having problems levitating. She struggled for a few days, and then woke up one morning to find she was totally incapable of levitating, and had to drag herself on the floor. She had been staying in abandoned structures for the past month and a half until two weeks back when she ran into Imoran in Ilaro forest.

"I need to talk to someone", Nimi said to herself.

Talking to Malika was out of the question. For the sake of her powers, she needed to do something urgently.

It was at this moment she realized how much she missed Omoyeni and Omitoni. If they were together, they could make the best of a situation, however bad it seemed.

Omitoni lived beyond **the seven seas** of Agbedemeji, while Omoyeni was a priest in a small town after **the seven mountains**. At this juncture, they were the only ones she could trust. The journey would be far from pleasant, but she was determined to talk to someone.

"I'll visit Omoyeni first, then we can make the trip together to Toni's place," she said to herself.

She tried to levitate and set out on her journey, but she fell. She tried again and still fell. She looked at Imoran and started to cry. A bird flew very close to her, stared at her curiously with beady eyes, and then fluttered its wings and dashed off, leaving her on the same spot.

She continued to cry and dragged herself off the path to rest her back on a mango tree.
The sun was setting already, and Imoran, her spirit dog, was nowhere to be found. She gave up hope and decided to get back to the uncompleted training school since it was just a short distance away.

Clip-clop, clip-clop! It was the sound of a horse coming out of the thick forest behind her, with Aja right behind it, trying to keep up.

She smiled and closed her eyes to feel the breeze as she believed that her problems were gradually evaporating. She needed to believe what she felt was real.

She would see Omoyeni soon. She didn't know it yet, but Omoyeni had felt a need to see her as well and had planned to take a trip in a few days, just that Omoyeni needed to go home first because she too had been away from her home for several years now.

12

OMOYENI'S TRIP

The path was lonely and quiet but Omoyeni was familiar with the road. She had walked that route before and had passed through that stretch of the road so many times. She could practically walk the road with her eyes closed. Even the trees, shrubs, and weeds know her by name.

The atmosphere was different from what she was used to at Agbedemeji. Though her land was far beyond the mountains, a lot of other creatures, most especially humans have tried to gain access to Omoke, the famous last village, but the protector had hidden the village behind a cloak.

It seemed just like yesterday that she was sent to Agbedemeji. She was sent there seven days after she clocked seven years old.

As she breathed in and out, she could feel the weight of the responsibilities that awaited her, yet her face spelled excitement.

A strange wind blew across her. She dismissed it and ran towards home. She was just a few steps away from her guardian's house; the place she called home.

Two elderly women walked past her, and she greeted them.

"That lady looks so much like Omoyeni, the one from the protector's clan", one of the women said. "You were young when they left the village in pursuit of more powers", said the second woman. The strange wind blew even stronger and Omoyeni felt attracted to the source of water, the stream they all used. The stream was said to be an extension of the one at Agbedemeji.

The two women thought she was following them, but she hurriedly ran past them. The river had overrun its banks and was about to cause a flood. She spread her arms and pushed forth with all her strength, pushing back the floodwaters back into the river. Her feet slid backward by a few feet as the water pushed back at her. The water was strong, but she was stronger. She created another path for the water with her left hand and directed the water towards it.

The women stood in awe, with their mouths agape. They were surprised. It would have shocked them to know that Omoyeni could read their minds. She merely smiled and left them at the river. She went home and was welcomed. She had returned after spending eleven years at a place nobody from her clan knew. Everyone was happy.

While celebrating her at her home, the women who had witnessed what she did went on to tell others what they had seen.

"That felt good." Omoyeni thought to herself.
She had never felt that way before - the adrenaline rush, the feeling of saving a group of people. At that point, she did not remember any of what she had been taught at Agbede Meji. All she knew was that she was not going to watch idly while the whole village got wiped out because a riverine queen got angry for some unknown reason.

With joy in her heart, she went back on her route and continued her journey. Omoyeni walked down the slopy hill which would lead her to the only house around that part of the village - her first teacher's house.

No one had ever seen the face of the most powerful individual in the village. At least that was what she called herself, but I know what she looks like. "Yemoja protects me," Omoyei whispered.

Omoyeni was only a few steps away from the isolated hut when the weather became windy. She could feel its presence.

"And where do you think you are going?" Omo the high priestess asked
"I wanted…" Omoyeni tried to explain.
"Shut up!" Omo cuts in.
"You cannot leave this place for eleven years and expect a big party to celebrate your return. Who do you think you are? Eledua? Those who told you that there is something special about you are deceiving you. You will never be welcomed here;

you should go back to where you are coming from."

Omoyeni was shocked and amazed when she heard this. She felt rejected by the one she looked up to. She wondered why the high priestess would say something like this because wasn't she the one that gave her parents the message from Eledumare that she was chosen to be a warrior high priestess?
Going to her father's house was the next thing on her mind. Although she didn't were that was, she intended to find out. She also really wanted to see Nimi, but she had to go home first.
"I'll visit Nimi as soon as I am done seeing my parents", she said to herself.

She hoped the warmth of home would help her get over the way she was feeling. If only she knew what awaited her at home.

13

HELP ALONG THE WAY

With her eyes still closed, Nimi could hear the horse draw closer. She opened her eyes in excitement. The horse had a man on its back and Imoran was running behind them, trying to keep up. This made Nimi very amused because Imoran could not keep up at all. He kept trying as hard as he could, but was not doing a good job of it.

"I come bringing help", said Imoran.
"*Bawo ni ara re?*" (How are you feeling?)
"*Se o tile dide?*" (Can you levitate now?)
"Imoran, you know I don't understand the language you are speaking, so why bother to speak it?"
"One can only hope," replied Imoran.
"Stop being so dramatic, Imoran. Let's focus on what is ahead of us at this moment. Who is this and where did you find them?" said Nimi.

"Good question! I was looking for help so that we can remain unnoticed, because you would have to agree with me that a young woman floating two feet off the ground is not normal, to say the least. *Abi Kini o ro?* (What do you think?)"

"Frustrating me is not in your best interest Imoran. I have warned you o, and please remember that my powers have been acting anyhow they like, so I don't scorch the fur off your body, so to speak."

While all this was going on, the man and his horse stared and wondered at what this dog and the young girl were doing.

The man wondered why his horse brought him to this place. He wondered what he could do to help the young lady on the floor leaning against a tree. He was concerned; he hoped she hadn't hurt herself badly. As he stared at this young lady whose skin was like the bright sun and who appeared fitter than any girl he had ever seen, he got down from his horse and walked towards her.

"Hello! My name is Goke, the son of Ajani the hunter. I would like to help you if you don't mind. Are you hurt?"

Nimi ignored him as if he wasn't there, then turned to Imoran and asked: "How can he help me? If he finds out that I levitate instead of walking, what will happen? How will he react?"

Imran replied: "I think you can just tell him that you can't move your legs." {All these conversations were going on via their minds}

Turning to Goke, Nimi looked him in the eyes and asked "How can you help me? Can you give me your legs? Will you be my legs? Will you walk for me?"

With a smile on his face, Goke bent down and said: "if it will make your eyes light up, then I will give all to you."
Nimi, wanting to know what was on his mind, then went ahead to read his mind and she was shocked at his thoughts.

"Oh! Why is this girl wasting my time? I have somewhere to be. We need a priestess to help my father. If not that I was told to go to where the horse leads then I won't be here. I would be on my way to the protected village. By the way, I wonder why it is called the protected village. What is so special about this village that nobody can find it? Everybody has been looking for this village all this while, and yet no one has found it. This girl is wasting my time. I wish she would just tell me what she wants me to do."

Nimi was shocked because he was referring to Omoyeni's village. He didn't know where it was; come to think of it, neither did she. She needed to go and see her friend. How was she going to do that? In her heart, she thought that he finally had some use. He was the only one who could help since her powers were out of work. She couldn't float and she couldn't use most of her other powers. She was lucky that she could still use her mind-reading power - that seemed to be the only thing that still worked well for her.

Nimi was afraid, scared that she would never be able to use her powers again.
"Well, you can help me by helping me on your horse and taking me as far as you can on your journey. I can't seem to use my legs, and I don't know what else to do."

"All right!" he said. "I will take you as far as I can but please don't be sad because I do not think that being sad will help us on this journey. As I have told you before, my name is Goke and I will be helping you throughout this journey."

THE END. Stay connected for Volume Two

GLOSSARY

Aja: Dog

Aseda o!:   An exclamation calling
the creator

Eledumare: God

Baa mi: My father

Agbedemeji Aye: Midway between Earth

Orirun: Source

Ibusun: Bed

Iya Ewe: Mother of all children

Se ara e ya: Are you fine?

"Wo Malika, ma je kin wo oju e o!": look Malik, don't
let me get angry with you

Bawo ni ara re: How are you feeling?

Se o tile dide?:   Can you stand now?

Abi kini o ro?:	What do you think?
Akada:	Student